# DISNEY

# CLUB PENGUIN™

# PH's Great Puffle Search

## PICK YOUR PATH 7

by Tracey West

Grosset & Dunlap

An Imprint of Penguin Group

GROSSET & DUNLAP
Published by the Penguin Group
Penguin Group (USA) Inc., 375 Hudson Street, New York,
New York 10014, USA
Penguin Group (Canada), 90 Eglinton Avenue East, Suite 700,
Toronto, Ontario M4P 2Y3, Canada
(a division of Pearson Penguin Canada Inc.)
Penguin Books Ltd., 80 Strand, London WC2R 0RL, England
Penguin Group Ireland, 25 St. Stephen's Green, Dublin 2, Ireland
(a division of Penguin Books Ltd.)
Penguin Group (Australia), 250 Camberwell Road, Camberwell,
Victoria 3124, Australia
(a division of Pearson Australia Group Pty. Ltd.)
Penguin Books India Pvt. Ltd., 11 Community Centre, Panchsheel Park,
New Delhi—110 017, India
Penguin Group (NZ), 67 Apollo Drive, Rosedale, Auckland 0632, New Zealand
(a division of Pearson New Zealand Ltd.)
Penguin Books (South Africa) (Pty.) Ltd., 24 Sturdee Avenue,
Rosebank, Johannesburg 2196, South Africa

Penguin Books Ltd., Registered Offices:
80 Strand, London WC2R 0RL, England

© 2012 Disney. All rights reserved. Used under license by
Penguin Young Readers Group. Published by Grosset & Dunlap, a division of
Penguin Young Readers Group, 345 Hudson Street, New York, New York 10014.
GROSSET & DUNLAP is a trademark of Penguin Group (USA) Inc.
Printed in the U.S.A.

ISBN 978-0-448-46149-6          10 9 8 7 6 5 4 3 2

"I'm so excited," you say, pushing open the door to the Pet Shop. "I can't believe I'm going to adopt my first puffle!"

"Puffles are awesome," says your good friend Jet, a light blue penguin wearing a puffle T-shirt and red sneakers. "I just got my puffle, Fluffy, a few days ago, and already I feel like we're best friends."

Jet has been begging you to explore Club Penguin with him for the last two weeks, and you finally visited the island a few days ago. So far, you've been exploring all the different things there are to do. You've been playing games and meeting new friends—and everyone seems to have a puffle. Now you're anxious to get one of your own.

"Wow," you say, looking around. The Pet Shop is a bright and colorful place with lots of stuff going on. Large plastic tubes wind all around the shop, and you can see fuzzy puffles bouncing through them. There's puffle furniture on display and shelves filled with what looks like puffle food.

But the most exciting thing in the shop is the little hut where the puffles hang out.

Some of the puffles are happily playing on carpeted towers, while others are lounging in comfy puffle beds. You start counting all the different colors you see.

"Black, pink, white, red, orange, brown, yellow, blue, purple, and green," you say. "Ten different colors! That's ten different kinds of puffles to choose from."

"They all have different personalities, too," Jet explains, "and different talents. Like, Fluffy is a blue puffle, and it likes to play ball."

"I like to play ball, too," you say. "Maybe I should get a blue puffle."

"But you also like to eat stuff, like orange puffles do," Jet points out. "And you like to jump on trampolines, like a pink puffle. It's kind of hard to decide."

"So how did you do it?" you ask.

Jet points to a wood pedestal next to the puffle hut. There's a thick purple book on it. "I read the Puffle Handbook."

You waddle over to the book and start to read.
*"What Is a Puffle?*

*Puffles are small, round, furry creatures. They make great pets! Most species are native to*

6

*the wilds of Club Penguin, although some have been discovered elsewhere."*

The book has information about each type of puffle. There's a lot of stuff to think about. When you close the book, you are more confused than before.

"I wish I could adopt all ten of them!" you say. "But that's a lot of puffles to take care of. I should probably start with one and see how it goes."

A penguin walks into the Pet Shop, and the other penguins there get excited and start to run toward her. She's a light brown penguin with freckled cheeks and long brown hair. She's wearing a bright purple vest with a light purple safari hat. There's a turquoise backpack on her back and a whistle around her neck.

"Hey," you say. "She looks familiar. Didn't I just read something about her in *The Club Penguin Times*?"

Jet nods. "That's PH. She's, like, the biggest puffle expert on Club Penguin. She knows everything there is to know about puffles. You should talk to her."

"I don't know," you reply. "She looks kind of busy."

PH is talking in a cheerful voice to all the penguins gathered around her.

"PH, how do know what kind of food is best to feed your puffle?" a penguin is asking her.

"Well, you can never go wrong with some good old O'berries," PH replies with a smile. "But if you're not sure, just look at your puffle's face when you try to feed it. If it smiles, that means it likes the food you're giving it."

"Thanks, PH!" the penguin replies.

"Happy to help, mate!" she says. "Now, I heard through the O'berry line that there's trouble with the *Puffle Launch* game, and I came to check it out."

"Go talk to her," Jet urges you. "I hear she's really friendly."

You shyly approach PH. "Um, excuse me, PH?" you say.

She turns to you and smiles. "G'day! You look more curious than a brown puffle in a gadget shop. Do you have a question?"

"Actually, yes," you say. "I want to adopt my first puffle, but they're all so different that I can't decide which one to get. I was wondering if maybe you could give me some tips on how to learn more about puffles. My friend Jet says you're an expert."

Behind you, Jet waves at her with a starstruck look on his face.

"I may be an expert, but I'm always learning new things about puffles," PH says, waving back at Jet. "And there's nothing I like better than yabbering on about puffles. I'll be happy to help you, just as soon as I check out *Puffle Launch*."

She waddles over to an alcove on the other side of the shop that holds a large gray cannon with red trim. The cannon is aimed out the open window. You look up and notice an opening in the plastic tubing overhead that will allow puffles to drop into the cannon.

PH fiddles with the cannon for a few minutes and comes back out, wiping her flippers on a rag.

"Just needed a little O'berry grease," she says. "Would you like me to show you how to play *Puffle Launch*? That's an ace way to find out some of the things puffles can do. After that I've got to embark on an exciting expedition into the wilderness to study puffles in the wild. I've got a lead on some interesting puffle behavior."

Playing *Puffle Launch* sounds like fun to you, but before you can answer, Jet whispers in your ear. "Ask if we can go on the expedition with her! That would be awesome."

If you ask if you can go on the expedition with her, go to page 36.

If you ask PH to show you how to play *Puffle Launch*, go to page 68.

# CONTINUED FROM PAGE 18.

Jet likes your idea. "That would be awesome if she would let us go on a secret EPF mission with her. Let's see what she says!"

You and Jet hurry back down the path and quickly catch up with PH. She looks surprised to see you.

"We'd like to help," you say. "If that's okay."

PH grins. "That's an ace attitude, mates! Sure, you two can come along. But if things get dangerous, I'll have to ask you to hang back and let me handle it."

"Dangerous?" you ask nervously.

"It's probably nothing," PH says. "But if Herbert is involved, things can sometimes get a bit bonkers."

"I think I've heard of Herbert," Jet says. "He's a polar bear, right?"

PH nods. "Ever since he came to the island, he's made it his mission to take down the EPF," she says. "He might not even be involved this time, but you never know. One of our Elite Puffles is missing. Its name is Chirp."

"I didn't know puffles could be part

of the EPF," you say.

"Sure they are, mates! Puffles are an important part of the EPF," PH replies. "G says that Chirp was last seen at the Ski Lodge. That's where we're headed."

When you get to the Ski Lodge, PH searches the surrounding snow.

"Beauty!" she cries. "Puffle tracks. Let's follow them."

The three of you follow the tracks across the snow and into the mountains of Club Penguin. The tracks lead right to what looks like the mouth of a cave that's blocked with a big rock.

PH frowns thoughtfully. "Hmm. Did it get into the cave somehow?"

You kneel down and examine the rock. "There's room under here for a puffle to squeeze through—but not a penguin."

PH grins. "No worries!" She blows the whistle around her neck, and moments later, a purple puffle arrives.

"Pop, we need to move this boulder," PH says.

"How can a tiny puffle move a big boulder?"

12

Jet wonders out loud, and soon you all find out.

Pop produces a bubble wand and starts to blow a bubble. It gets bigger . . . and bigger . . . and bigger, until the ginormous bubble is larger than the boulder. It surrounds the rock and floats it up and out of the way.

"Awesome!" you and Jet say.

"Thanks, Pop," PH says with a grin.

Pop hops away, and you, Jet, and PH enter the dark cave. You follow a tunnel that leads to a strange-looking metal doorway. There's a control panel with flashing shapes on the door, as well as a big red button.

**If you press the button, go to page 38.**

**If you decide to figure out the code on the dial, go to page 64.**

## CONTINUED FROM PAGE 63.

"Let's keep following the tracks," you say. "I have a feeling they're going to lead to something interesting."

"You're right," PH says, looking up at the sun. "The snow is melting quickly. We'd better follow the tracks while we can."

You all continue on the trail, following the tracks until you come to a large, leafy tree.

Jet looks up. "The puffle might have climbed the tree," he guesses.

"Maybe not," you say, pointing. "Look!"

There's a hole in the dirt beneath the roots of the tree.

"Would you get a look at that?" PH says, kneeling down. "Maybe it's some kind of underground habitat."

"So where do we look next?" Jet asks.

If you decide to climb down the hole, go to page 29.

If you climb up the tree, go to page 79.

## CONTINUED FROM PAGE 39.

You exit the cave and blow the whistle twice.
*Tweet! Tweet!* The loud sound echoes off
the mountains.

You and Jet anxiously scan the horizon,
hoping it worked. Then you see a tiny pink ball of
fluff bouncing across the snow to you.

"Over here!" you yell as the pink puffle gets
closer. "PH is inside the cave! She fell into a hole!
It's some kind of trap!"

The pink puffle nods and hops past you, and
you and Jet follow it into the cave. It examines
the hole and then produces a lasso and begins to
swing it expertly.

"Cool!" you say.

The puffle throws the lasso down the hole.
You and Jet run to help it. You grab on to the end
of the rope, steadying it. Then you feel a tug on
the other end.

A few seconds later, PH emerges from the
hole, carrying a yellow puffle in her backpack.

"Thanks, Loop!" she tells the pink puffle.
Then she smiles at you and Jet. "Beauty of a
rescue, mates. It was smart to use the whistle."

15

"Is that Chirp?" you ask, nodding at the yellow puffle.

"Sure is," PH says. "Chirp spotted Herbert outside the Ski Village and it followed him to the cave. But she fell into his trap, just like I did. Now, let's get back to HQ and write up a report."

You and Jet have never been inside EPF headquarters, and you're amazed by all the blinking machines and secret agents waddling around. A blue penguin in a lab coat and glasses approaches you.

"PH has told me about your work in the field," G says. "I am happy to give you each a medal."

You look at the medal, which is shaped like a puffle.

"Awesome!" you say. "Now all I need is a real puffle!"

## THE END

## CONTINUED FROM PAGE 70.

You aim for the green balloon, and the red puffle bounces up, then bounces again, a little higher . . . and a little higher . . . you did it! The puffle goes through the flaming hoop.

"That was ace!" PH congratulates you. "You're a real natural at this."

"Thanks!" you say, feeling proud.

"So, I was thinking," PH says. "You'll probably learn better if we go find some puffles doing the things they like to do. Which would you like to see first? We can check out some yellow puffles at the Stage, or go see some white puffles at the Iceberg."

**If you choose white puffles at the Iceberg, go to page 35.**

**If you choose yellow puffles at the Stage, go to page 43.**

## CONTINUED FROM PAGE 37.

You decide to keep quiet about the green puffle, just in case it was a leaf after all. You hurry to catch up to PH and Jet.

Suddenly you hear a ringing, and PH takes a black phone out of her jacket pocket.

"Yes, G?" she asks. "Um-hum. Um-hum. Yes, I see. I'll be right there."

PH shuts off the phone and turns to you and Jet. "Sorry, mates, but I've got to run. EPF business." She waddles back down the path before you can say anything.

"Maybe we should go with her and see if she needs help," you suggest.

"Or we could try to impress her," Jet says. "Let's keep heading north and see if we can catch up with that mysterious herd of puffles."

**If you and Jet chase after her, go to page 11.**

**If you and Jet keep heading north, go to page 67.**

18

## CONTINUED FROM PAGE 66.

You reach for one of the wires, a red one, and yank it out.

The chamber begins to vibrate, knocking you off your feet. The ceiling opens up and a steel cage drops down, protecting the machine.

"Another booby trap!" PH yells.

Before you can get up and run, the floor underneath opens up. You, Jet, PH, and Chirp go sliding down a metal chute at rocket speed. The chute twists and turns through a dark cavern, and then suddenly you're blinded by sunlight as it spits you out into the snow.

*Whomp!* You hit the snow hard and glide across the open snowy field in front of you.

"What happened?" you ask when you come to a stop.

"Herbert protected his machine with a booby trap," PH explains. "And that chute seems to have deposited us far away from the cave. I'm not even sure where we are."

You frown. "I'm sorry. We didn't destroy the machine!"

PH smiles. "Don't worry, mate. I know the

19

coordinates of the cave, so we can get some more Agents on the case right away. And the important thing is, we saved Chirp!"

Chirp hops over to you, smiling. Then it begins to play a happy song on its flute. The song is so happy that you and Jet can't help yourselves—you start to dance.

"This turned out to be a pretty cool adventure," Jet says. "But you still need to adopt a puffle."

"I know," you say. "Let's go back to the Pet Shop! I want to play with all of them before I decide."

## THE END

## CONTINUED FROM PAGE 63.

"We may never get another chance to see this dance again," you point out. "Maybe we should stay and watch."

PH nods. "All right. But let's duck behind this O'berry bush. I don't want to disturb them."

The three of you crouch behind the bush and watch the puffles dance. They've formed a circle, and they hop around the circle first to the right and then to the left. Then the puffles take turns hopping into the middle of the circle, one by one, as the other puffles circle them. You notice that the purple puffle in the group seems to be the best dancer.

PH records the scene with a video camera, whispering as she films. "It looks like a dance, but it might also be some kind of game," she says. "Or are they telling a story? I need to check and see if any patterns form."

The puffles all hop into the circle, and then all of them hop out again. That seems to be the end of the dance because the puffles all nod to one another and hop off in different directions.

PH stands up. "This is some top footage

21

right here! I can't wait to get back to my igloo and study it."

"What about the strange tracks?" Jet asks.

"Oh, right!" PH says. You all go back to where you spotted the last track, but the warm sun has melted it into a puddle.

"We've lost the trail," she says. "But I've logged the coordinates, so I can come back someday."

Then she frowns. "Oh, I forgot! You were supposed to learn about puffles on this trip so you could choose one of your own. Sorry I couldn't help you, mate."

"But you did," you assure her. "When we get back I'm going to adopt a purple puffle. I feel like dancing!"

## THE END

## CONTINUED FROM PAGE 28.

You hop into the box that looks like a door—
and immediately find yourself standing
in the middle of town!

"How did that happen?" you wonder.

Jet walks up to you.

"Hey," you say. "What happened in there?
And where's PH?"

Jet looks confused. "In where?" he asks.
"And how should I know where PH is? Probably
studying puffles somewhere."

Now you're confused. "Weren't we just in the
Box Dimension together? So PH could teach us
about orange puffles?"

Jet puts a flipper on your forehead. "Are you
feeling okay?"

"Yes," you reply with a sigh. But really,
you're not. Something weird must have happened
in the Box Dimension. And now your adventure
is over!

## THE END

"Let's try the O'berry paste," you suggest.

The thick paste plugs the hole just fine, and the three of you climb into the rowboat. You and Jet row the boat across the bay. When you land, you eagerly enter the cave. You've never seen the brown-puffle cave before.

Inside, the cave is like nothing you've ever imagined. It's filled with dozens of machines with computer screens; wires; strange, twisting tubes; and canisters filled with liquids of all colors. Each machine is being worked on by brown puffles, some of them wearing safety glasses.

"Hello there!" PH calls out. Some of the brown puffles look up and smile, but one group is so busy working on something that they don't even notice you. The machine they're busy with is making a weird whirring sound—just like the sound you heard outside.

You and Jet follow PH as she approaches the puffles.

"Excuse me," she says politely. "Do you mind showing us this machine you're working on?"

The three brown puffles stop and smile when

they see PH. They hop up and down, trying to explain what they're doing.

PH seems to understand them a little. "I think they're trying to tell us that this machine makes something," she says. "They want us to help them try it out."

One of the puffles hops over to a metal panel on the front of the machine. There are two levers on the panel—a green one and a blue one. The puffle hops back and forth between them.

"I think it wants us to pull one of the levers," PH says.

"But which one?" you ask.

**If you pull the green lever, go to page 34.**

**If you pull the blue lever, go to page 62.**

"Come on," you urge. "Let's give this scrap wood a try."

"Well, my O'berry paste has never failed me," PH says. "But I like your inventive spirit. Let's do it!"

Jet helps you find a piece of scrap wood to fit over the hole in the boat, and you even find some stray nails at the base of the dock. You use a rock to hammer the nails and patch up the hole.

"Looks good," you say. "Let's push off!"

You, Jet, and PH jump into the boat and begin to row across the bay—but you don't get far before water begins to pour in around the patch you've made.

"Quick! Row back to the dock!" PH urges, but it's too late. The boat is heavy with the three of you in it and quickly fills with water.

"We're sinking!" you cry.

PH blows the whistle around her neck. Moments later, a motorboat comes roaring into the bay with a Rescue Squad penguin at the helm and a red puffle bouncing by her side.

"That response time was ace, Blast," PH

tells the puffle as the squad member pulls you safely on board the motorboat.

"The puffle's name is Blast?" you ask.

PH nods. "It works for the EPF as part of the Elite Puffle Squad. We agents would be lost without them. Blast here heard my whistle and got us the help we needed."

You gaze at Blast, impressed.

"Sorry, mates, but it looks like our adventure is over for now," PH says.

"That's all right," you reply. "At least we got to meet a real EPF puffle!"

**THE END**

## CONTINUED FROM PAGE 42.

"The Box Dimension sounds cool," you say. "I've never been there."

You go to Jet's igloo, where he has a box portal. It looks like an ordinary cardboard box on the floor. But when you waddle closer, you see that it's filled with a weird whirling, swirling purple energy.

"Jump in!" Jet urges you. "We'll follow."

You take a deep breath and hop in the box. The next thing you know, you're in a world of cardboard boxes floating in an eerie, purple haze.

Suddenly, you see an orange puffle stick its head out of a box. You jump after it, but it disappears. Then you see a bigger box beside you—and it kind of looks like a door.

**If you go through the big box that looks like a door, go to page 23.**

**If you follow the orange puffle, go to page 47.**

# CONTINUED FROM PAGE 14.

"An underground habitat! Cool!" you say. "I've got to see this. Let me get down there."

"That's an ace idea, but—" PH begins, but it's too late. You get on your belly, planning on sliding into the hole the same way you'd slide across the ice. But you're only halfway through the hole when you get stuck!

"—you might not fit," PH finishes.

"No problem! I can squeeze right out!" you call, but your voice sounds muffled in the hole. You push with all your might, but to your dismay, you don't budge at all. You're really stuck.

"Nothing a little O'berry grease can't fix," you hear PH say, and then she begins to slather the orange goo around the opening of the hole. You start to laugh.

"It tickles!" you say.

"Give it another try," PH suggests.

You squeeze . . . and squeeze . . . and then . . . *pop!* You slide right back out.

"Wow, you're right," you say. "That O'berry grease works great."

"It was a good try," PH tells you. "But I'm afraid if a puffle did go down that hole it's probably good and scared right now. I'm going to log the coordinates of the location and come back another time with a special robot camera that I can send down the hole."

You're disappointed. "So does that mean this adventure is over?"

"Well, for today," PH says. "But you should keep on learning about puffles on your own. You're curious, and that's a good quality to have when you're studying puffles. I think you and Jet would make ace puffle handlers someday."

You and Jet look at each other and smile. You just got a compliment from PH, and she's an expert!

**THE END**

# CONTINUED FROM PAGE 67.

"I used to be a member of the Rescue Squad," Jet tells you. "Trust me. Moss grows on the north side of a tree, and we need to go right."

You've never heard of the Rescue Squad before, but you know that it's pointless to argue with Jet.

"Fine," you say. "Let's go right."

You and Jet make your way through the forest, the snow crunching under your feet as you waddle along. The path goes on and on and on, and after a while you begin to wonder if you've made the right decision. Jet is unsure, too.

"Maybe we should head back," he says. "I'm pretty sure we're heading north, but I don't see any sign of that puffle herd."

You nod your head in agreement. "Yeah, there's no . . . puffles!" You shout the last word.

"Right. No puffles," Jet repeats.

"No, I mean, PUFFLES!" you say loudly. "Look!"

There's an intersecting path up ahead and traveling on it are puffles of every color. They're hopping along, and they just keep coming and coming.

"There must be dozens—no, hundreds of them," Jet says.

"Where are they going?" you wonder.

"Let's catch up!" Jet suggests, racing ahead of you.

You join the puffle throng, marveling at the size of the herd. You've never seen so many in one place. The puffles are moving swiftly, and soon you leave the trees behind and come to the edge of the island. The blue ocean stretches out in front of you.

But even more amazing than the sparkling ocean and the herd of puffles is the light show happening on the horizon. Blue and green lights are swirling and dancing against a dark purple sky. The puffles sway back and forth, enjoying the incredible beauty.

"Is it fireworks?" Jet asks.

"No," you reply. "I've heard about this. It's natural, and it's called an aurora borealis. It has something to do with charged particles in the atmosphere. Isn't it amazing?"

Jet takes out a camera. "We should record this for PH."

"Make sure you get footage of the puffles, too."

The natural light show goes on for what seems like hours. Then the pulsing lights begin to fade, and the puffle herd slowly begins to meander away.

"Let's get back to town," you suggest. "We've got to find PH and tell her what we've seen."

Luck is with you, because when you return to town you spot PH coming out of the Coffee Shop.

"Hey, PH!" you yell. "We've got something to show you."

You race up to PH, and Jet holds up his camera. The puffle handler's eyes grow wide.

"How did you get this?" she asks.

You explain that you and Jet traveled north and found the puffle herd. PH is impressed.

"This discovery is a real beauty," she says. "It could mean that puffles can predict when an aurora borealis is about to happen."

She tells Aunt Arctic about your discovery, and the next day you and Jet are on the cover of *The Club Penguin Times*!

"We can't stop here," you tell Jet. "Our days of exploring Club Penguin have just begun!"

**THE END**

**CONTINUED FROM PAGE 25.**

"I think I'll try the green lever," you say.

You pull the lever. The machine grunts and pulses. You hear a creaking sound above your head and look up to see a giant metal drum opening up.

*Splat!* Gallons and gallons of gooey marshmallows cascade out of the drum, completely drenching you!

"Help!" you cry.

Jet rushes to help you and pushes up the green lever. The drum closes—but not before he is covered in icky, sticky marshmallows, too.

The brown puffles hop around, excited. You're not sure—was that supposed to happen?

PH shakes her head, and you can tell she's trying not to laugh—but you wouldn't blame her if she did. You and Jet look pretty funny!

"That's quite the mess you're in!" she says. "Better head back to your igloos and get cleaned up. Maybe we can try this again some other time."

You're disappointed, but you have no choice. You're a big marshmallowy mess!

**THE END**

## CONTINUED FROM PAGE 17.

"Let's go to the Iceberg," you say.

When you get to the Iceberg, you see some white puffles hopping around. There are also a bunch of penguins on one side of the Iceberg wearing hardhats and drilling.

"It's a tipping party!" Jet cries. "I've heard that if enough penguins get on the Iceberg and drill, it will tip into the water."

"Let's try it!" you say eagerly.

You and Jet join the party and start drilling. You quickly get bored and start to watch the white puffles sliding on the ice.

You leave the party and approach PH, who's studying the puffles.

"I think I'd like to adopt a white puffle," you tell her.

PH nods. "Good choice. They're a little bit shy, but they're real aces when it comes to outdoor sports."

"Thanks, PH," you say. "I never could have made a decision without you!"

## THE END

## CONTINUED FROM PAGE 10.

You'd normally be too shy to ask PH to go on the expedition, but it sounds amazing. And the worst she can say is no, right?

"Um, excuse me, PH," you say nervously. "But maybe Jet and I could help you with your expedition? I bet that would be a good way for us to learn about puffles."

PH is thoughtful for a moment. Finally, she grins. "I think that's a beaut of an idea!" she says. She pats her purple backpack. "I'm always busy taking photos and notes when I'm out in the field. But I worry that I'm going to miss something. If you mates come with me I'll have four extra eyes and four extra flippers to work with."

Jet salutes her. "Our eyes and flippers are at your service!"

PH laughs. "Bonza! Then let's get started. One of Gary's weather balloons picked up an image of a large group of puffles traveling north. It's unusual behavior for puffles, and I want to check it out."

She leads you and Jet out of the Pet Shop to the Forest. Snow crunches under your webbed feet as you make your way through the tall evergreen trees.

"I've heard of puffles gathering for parties and celebrations," PH explains as you go. "But according to Gary, they're traveling over a long distance. It's pretty exciting. This could be a new discovery."

The path forks, and PH motions for you to go left. "North is this way," she says, looking at a compass.

You're about to turn when something green whizzes by you and shoots down the right-hand path. For a second you're sure it's a green puffle flying with a propeller hat, but it vanishes into the trees. Maybe it was just a leaf, caught by the wind.

You stop, wondering if you should tell PH.

**If you follow PH down the left-hand path, go to page 18.**

**If you tell PH that you think you saw a green puffle, go to page 60.**

# CONTINUED FROM PAGE 13.

"Interesting," PH says. "Looks like Chirp was onto something. I wonder what's behind the door?"

"I bet this red button opens it," you say, hitting it with your flipper.

"No!" PH cries, but she's too late. Instead of opening the door, the button opens up the floor right underneath PH's feet.

*Whoosh!* PH falls through the trapdoor. Panicked, you and Jet kneel down and peer into the hole. It's pitch-dark, and you can't see a thing.

"PH?" you call down, but she doesn't answer you.

Your heart is pounding. "Oh no! What have I done? What if Herbert is down there, waiting to eat her for dinner?"

"I think he's a vegetarian," Jet tells you. "Anyway, we should keep calm. What would PH do?"

"She'd probably use her whistle to call for help," you say. "But we don't have a whistle."

Jet waddles a few feet away. "Yes, we do," he

says, holding up a shiny silver whistle. "Look! It must have slipped off the chain when PH fell."

"So do we just blow it?" you ask. "Should we do it once or a bunch of times?"

> **If you blow the whistle two times, go to page 15.**
>
> **If you blow the whistle one time, go to page 73.**

## CONTINUED FROM PAGE 44.

"I've heard you can sometimes find green puffles at the Beacon," Jet says. "Those guys are funny. Let's go there."

A few minutes later you're climbing up the stairs of the red-and-white-striped Lighthouse that overlooks the island's coast. When you emerge onto the Beacon, a green puffle wearing a propeller hat is flying around the bright light.

"Green puffles love to zip around in their propeller hats," PH tells you. "They've got heaps of energy, and they're funny little rascals, too."

The fluffy green puffle flies right up to you, blows a raspberry with his tongue, and then zooms away. You laugh.

"I guess you're right," you say. "Hey, come back here!"

You and Jet run around the Beacon, chasing the green puffle, but it darts back and forth and you can't catch it. Jet finally gives up, and he hops up on a wood crate to look through the telescope.

"Hey, the *Migrator*'s here!" he calls out.

"Beauty!" PH exclaims. "Captain

Rockhopper's got an ace red-puffle story for you, mates. Let's go see him."

You climb down the Lighthouse and outside you see that the *Migrator* is anchored at the dock. On the deck, a red penguin with a black beard and a pirate hat is carrying a heavy crate from belowdecks.

"No way. It's really Rockhopper!" Jet cries, excited. "I've always wanted to meet him."

As you all race up the gangplank, Captain Rockhopper notices PH. "Ahoy there, lass," he says, putting down the crate. "Ye be PH, right? How be the puffles on Club Penguin?"

"They're as fascinating as ever," PH replies. "I was hoping you could tell my mates here how you brought red puffles to the island."

"Aye, I can," the pirate replies. "So there I was, sailin' the seas in me trusty ship, when I found a red puffle lost at sea. I rescued it and it led me to the red puffles on Rockhopper Island. The little fellas were full o' piratey spirit, and they hopped aboard me ship and came to Club Penguin."

He nods over to the tall mast. "But the one I rescued became me true-blue friend.

41

That's me first mate, Yarr."

Yarr is bouncing up and down in the crow's nest on top of the mast. You wave to it, and it responds by shooting snowballs at you from a tiny cannon.

You and Jet dodge the snowballs, laughing. "Wow, Yarr is really cool," you say. "Maybe I should go adopt a red puffle."

"We still have more puffles to learn about," PH reminds you. "Where should we go next?"

**If you head to the Box Dimension, go to page 28.**

**If you head to the Snow Forts, go to page 51.**

# CONTINUED FROM PAGE 17.

"Let's go to the Stage," you say.

You and Jet follow PH next door to the Stage. Inside, the Stage is set with a waterfall cascading down a sandy hill and a wooden bridge that goes over a flowing stream. To the right of the waterfall is what looks like an ancient Egyptian temple with a statue of a golden puffle on a pedestal.

"It's *Quest for the Golden Puffle*! This play is bonza!" PH exclaims.

An orange penguin wearing an adventurer's costume is crossing the bridge. On the other side, a penguin wrapped up like a mummy is waddling toward her. Between them, a yellow puffle wearing a black director's cap is hopping up and down.

"Yellow puffles are very creative," PH tells you. "They love to paint and sculpt. And this one is directing the play."

"Pretty impressive," you say. "I bet we'd have fun putting on plays together."

"Let's waddle on over to the Night Club," PH says. "I'm sure we'll find some black puffles up in the Arcade."

The three of you waddle to the Night Club and head upstairs. The Lounge is filled with tables, chairs, video games, and an arcade game called *Hit the Target*!

A small group of black puffles are hanging out there. Two of them are skateboarding around the circle pattern on the smooth floor. Two others are hurling snowballs at the targets in the game.

"Cool!" Jet cries, and he runs up to shoot targets with the black puffles. You're entranced by the skateboarding puffles—these guys are really good!

"I bet I could learn a lot of tricks from them," you say.

"We've still got more puffles to check out," PH says. "Where to next, mate?"

If you choose the Beacon, go to page 40.

If you choose the Stadium, go to page 56.

# CONTINUED FROM PAGE 76.

"Let's keep chasing the green puffle," you say. "I have a feeling that he's going to lead us to that special O'berry bush."

"You may be right," PH agrees. "Let's go!"

You race through the trees as the green puffle whizzes through the Forest. Finally, he stops in a clearing, hovering above a bush. Huffing and puffing, you reach him.

Shiny, black O'berries are hanging off every branch of the bush. The green puffle flies up to one and gulps it down.

"Black O'berries!" PH says, gently handling one with her flipper. "They seem to be genuinely black, not old or rotten. This is a real discovery!"

She opens her turquoise backpack and pulls out a sterile plastic jar with a lid and some tweezers. Then she carefully plucks several berries and puts them in the jar. Next she takes out another jar and gathers some leaf samples. Then she cuts off one branch and places it in a third jar.

"I've got to get this back to my igloo and put it in water," she explains. "I want to see

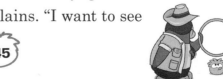

if I can grow the bush. But before we go, some photos!"

PH snaps photos of the bush from every angle. Then she turns to you and Jet.

"I think we're done here," she says. "I've got to get back. Thank you both for your help. If it weren't for you, this green puffle would never have led us to these black O'berries."

"Thanks," you say.

PH grins. "In fact, once I finish this report I will make sure you're listed as my co-O'berry discoverers. What do you think of that, mates?"

You and Jet look at each other and grin.

"That would be puffle-tastic!" you both reply.

## THE END

**CONTINUED FROM PAGE 28.**

You follow the orange puffle—and pop out of a completely different box! PH and Jet pop out of boxes on either side of you. Then the orange puffle suddenly appears in the box with you.

"They're fascinating," PH says, writing down notes. "They seamlessly move through the Box Dimension. But how?"

You reach down and pick up the orange puffle. It starts sniffing your pockets, looking for food.

"I like it," you say. "Can I adopt it?"

"It's up to it," PH says.

You look down at the puffle. "What do you say? Do you want to come home with me?"

The orange puffle nods—and in the next instant, you're all instantly transported to your igloo!

"Amazing!" PH says, scribbling quickly.

"I'll say," you agree. "I've got my first puffle!"

**THE END**

## CONTINUED FROM PAGE 70.

You aim for the cannon. The red puffle lands inside the cannon, but the cannon spins to the right and shoots the puffle wildly into the sky. The puffle falls into the water and then swims back to you.

"Your game's over," PH tells you. "But you're off to a good start. Want to try again?"

Before you can answer, something rings in PH's pocket. She takes out a spy phone and answers it, listening. Then she quickly turns it off.

"Some black puffles need rescuing in the Mine!" she says. "Let's go!"

When you get to the Mine Shack, PH suits you up with some scuba gear and a wet suit.

"The water can get very cold," she warns. "When you find the black puffle, surround it with an air bubble, so you can bring it back safely."

With PH and Jet behind you, you walk inside a dark cavern in the mine, barely lit by lanterns. The cabin opens up to an underground pool with chunks of ice floating on top. In the distance you can see a black puffle shivering on one of the pieces of ice.

"I'll save you!" you call out. You dive into the freezing water and swim until you reach the black puffle. Then you surround it with an air bubble like PH told you.

You suddenly see a dark shadow passing underneath you. It's got a long, thin head and body and a dozen dangling tentacles. It's a giant squid!

Your heart is pounding, and you swim as fast as you can to shore before the squid sees you. When you land on shore, the puffle's bubble pops, and it happily hops away.

"That was exciting," you say. "But I think I've had enough adventure for one day. I think I'd like to go back to the Pet Shop and adopt a black puffle."

The three of you head back into the dark cavern. Suddenly, you feel something brush past your face. You glance back, and in the dim light you see what looks like a puffle with bat wings fly away. Is that possible?

"I have a feeling we have a lot more to learn about puffles!" you say.

**THE END**

"I like to play sports, so I'll say that I'm sporty," you reply.

"Then we can narrow it down to three choices," PH says. "Pink puffles are really active and love to exercise. White puffles love outdoor sports, like ice-skating. And blue puffles are playful. They're always up for a game of catch and are easy to please."

You think about your day. You had the best time having a snowball fight with those cute blue puffles.

"I think I'll go with a blue one," you say.

PH grins. "Then let's get you to the Pet Shop!"

A short while later you and Jet are hanging in your igloo with your blue puffle.

"I think I made the right choice," you say.

"And once you learn how to take care of this one, you can always get more," Jet reminds you.

You slap your flapper on your forehead.

"No way! I'll never be able to decide!"

**THE END**

# CONTINUED FROM PAGE 42.

"Mmm, let's go to the Snow Forts," you reply.

You, Jet, and PH say good-bye to Captain Rockhopper and Yarr and waddle off the *Migrator* and past the Stadium, until you reach the Snow Forts. One fort has a faded red flag, and the other has a faded blue one. The two forts face each other on a field of white snow. Overlooking the scene is the large snowball-powered clock that gives the date and official Club Penguin time.

A snowball goes whizzing past your ear and you quickly jump to the side, dodging it.

"Hey, who threw that?" you ask. You don't see any penguins around.

PH laughs and points to the blue fort, where a small group of blue puffles is hopping up and down. "Looks like some blue puffles are up for a snowball fight."

Jet races to the red fort. "To the red fort! Quick!"

By the time you catch up to Jet, he's already making snowballs and throwing them at the blue fort. You quickly scoop up some cold snow, make a snowball, and send it flying.

You and Jet are fast, but the blue puffles

are really awesome. A barrage of snowballs falls from the sky on top of you like rain. You and Jet collapse on the ground, laughing.

The blue puffles hop over to you, smiling.

"Besides being playful, blue puffles are very friendly and loyal," PH explains.

You and Jet sit up and begin to stroke the soft fur of the blue puffles.

"How cute!" says a voice behind you. "I should take a photo of this for *The Club Penguin Times.*"

It's Aunt Arctic, the editor in chief of the newspaper! You'd recognize her anywhere. She's a green penguin with glasses, freckles, and a little pink hat on her head. There's a pencil tucked behind her ear.

"Hello, Aunt Arctic," PH says. "I was just teaching these two penguins about puffles."

"Oh, how delightful!" Aunt Arctic says. "Perhaps I can help. I have several puffles in my igloo right now. Would you like to meet them?"

You and Jet look at each other. This is a once-in-a-lifetime chance.

"Of course!" you both say.

Aunt Arctic's igloo is small and cozy, with

a rocking chair in front of a roaring fireplace. There are several puffles hopping around the room, playing.

"Let's see," PH says. "Which puffles haven't we seen today? Oh, yes, here's a white one."

"It's inside now, but normally it likes to be out in the cold and snow," Aunt Arctic explains.

You notice a pink puffle bouncing up and down on a trampoline.

"Wow, that puffle has lots of energy," you remark.

PH nods. "Yes. Pink puffles love to exercise."

An orange puffle hops up onto the rocking chair and starts to munch on the pillow. Aunt Arctic shakes her head.

"You orange puffles are always hungry," she says. "Let me get you a cookie."

As she walks off, PH points to a brown puffle in the corner. The puffle is wearing safety glasses and mixing liquids in a beaker.

"And last but not least, the brown puffle," she says. "They're very inventive."

You feel like your head is spinning. "I wish I could adopt one of every puffle! They're all amazing."

PH looks thoughtful. "Good point. Tell you what. I'm going to say some words, and you tell me which best describe your personality."

**If you say you are adventurous and intense, go to page 57.**

**If you say you are sporty, go to page 50.**

**If you say you are creative, go to page 71.**

**If you say you are fun-loving, go to page 72.**

**CONTINUED FROM PAGE 67.**

"I'm pretty sure moss grows on the south side of a tree," you insist.

You and Jet turn down the left path and keep marching down the tree-lined trail. The trail twists and turns. After what seems like hours, you're tired and haven't seen any puffles.

"What's that smell?" Jet asks, sniffing the air.

"I think it's the Pizza Parlor," you say. "We must have ended up near the Plaza. Let's go!"

Suddenly hungry, the two of you race to the Pizza Parlor and order one pizza with extra fish.

"It's too bad," you say after gulping down a slice. "I guess I'll never learn about puffles now."

"Did you say puffles?" a penguin at a nearby table asks. "I can tell you about my puffle."

"Me too," says another penguin.

Soon you're chatting about puffles with all the penguins in the Pizza Parlor. Getting lost wasn't such a bad thing after all!

**THE END**

## CONTINUED FROM PAGE 44.

"Let's go to the Stadium," you suggest.

When you get to the arena, a few penguins are skating on the ice rink there. A pink puffle is in the stands, and it looks like it's practicing a cheerleading routine.

A black penguin skates up to you, and you realize it's your friend Ace.

"Hey!" he tells you and Jet. "We're playing a hockey game in five minutes. Where've you been?"

"I totally forgot!" you say. You turn to PH. "Thanks for your help, but I promised I'd play."

"No problem," PH says with a smile. "I need to get started on my expedition, anyway."

You're sad when PH waddles off because you think that you may never decide on a puffle. But something happens during the game. The pink puffle really impresses you with its cheerleading routine. When the game is over, you go right to the Pet Shop and adopt a pink puffle of your own.

"This is great," you tell Jet. "Now we'll always have someone to cheer us on!"

## THE END

## CONTINUED FROM PAGE 54.

"I think I'm adventurous and intense," you say.

PH nods. "Then we can narrow it down. A black puffle or red puffle would be great for you."

You remember watching the black puffles in the Arcade, and all those cool skateboarding tricks they knew. Then you think about Captain Rockhopper's red puffle, Yarr. You imagine going on adventures with your own red puffle.

"It's a tough choice," you say. "But I think I'll adopt a red puffle!"

"Then let's get back to the Pet Shop," PH says.

Moments later you are proudly waddling around Club Penguin with your new red puffle hopping by your side.

"I think you should name it Jet," Jet says.

"I was thinking of calling it Rocky, after Rockhopper," you say. You look down at your red puffle. "Do you like that, Rocky?"

Rocky smiles and hops up and down.

"Great!" you say. "Now let's go play with your cannon!"

## THE END

57

# CONTINUED FROM PAGE 76.

"A puffle with a tail would be a great discovery," you say. "Let's follow the tracks!"

"All right," PH agrees. "Let me just record our location, so I can look for the black O'berries some other time."

Soon you're waddling through the trees as PH expertly follows the puffle tracks. The trees begin to thin out and you arrive at a bay at the base of a tall cliff. A small rowboat bobs up and down on the water, tied to a dock that juts out from the land.

Across the bay you can see a cave in the mountainside. A strange, whirring sound floats out of the cave and travels across the water.

"What do you know?" PH remarks. "We found another way to get to the cave of the brown puffles. This is where they were first discovered."

"What's that strange noise coming from the cave?" you ask.

"I'm not sure," PH says. "But I think we should check it out. I want to make sure the brown puffles aren't in any trouble. Sometimes their experiments can go a bit wonky, if you know what I mean. I worry about them."

Jet walks across the dock and pulls on the rope to bring the boat closer. Then he frowns.

"There's a hole in the boat," he says. "And it doesn't look like there's another way to get across."

"Maybe we can fix it," you say.

"We can try," PH says. "I know more about puffles than I do about boats. But I think we can plug the hole with some O'berry paste."

You nod to some scraps of wood on the dock. "Or we could use that wood," you suggest.

**If you repair the hole with O'berry paste, go to page 24.**

**If you repair the hole with scraps of wood, go to page 26.**

**CONTINUED FROM PAGE 37.**

You decide that you might as well tell PH about the green puffle. It could be important.

"PH!" you say, running up to her. "I'm pretty sure I saw a green puffle fly up the path on the right. I mean, it might have been a leaf, but it looked like a puffle to me."

"Let's check it out!" PH says eagerly. "If you're right, this is a great chance to study the behavior of a green puffle in the wild."

The three of you change direction and head down the right-hand path. It's quiet, and you're worried that you made a mistake. But then you see a tree branch wave up ahead, and a green puffle flies out of the branches.

"There it is!" you cry, and you all hurry after the green puffle.

The path makes another turn and you wind up in a clearing loaded with bushes bearing orange O-shaped berries.

"O'berry bushes!" Jet exclaims.

PH nods. "Yes, they grow all over Club Penguin. Puffles love them. Look!"

Wild puffles of every color have gathered

around the bushes, munching on the berries. PH waddles over and plucks some and then hands them to you and Jet.

"Try them," she said. "I think they're delicious."

You pop an O'berry in your mouth. It's bitter, spicy, and not like anything you've ever tasted. You don't really like it.

"Wow!" you exclaim. "That's . . . something else."

"Orange O'berries are the most common," PH tells you. "But I've found pink ones and purples ones, too. I've got to do some research on these different O'berries."

While PH is talking, the green puffle that you followed flies up to you and drops something at your feet. You reach down to pick it up, and to your surprise, you see that it's a black O'berry.

"PH, I think you'd better see this!" you say.

**Go to page 75.**

## CONTINUED FROM PAGE 25.

"Let's try the blue lever." You pull it.

The machine whirs and hums. A scoop rises up and dumps a perfect mound of vanilla ice cream into a bowl resting on a pillar. The pillar rises and hits the ice cream, which then hits a balloon, popping it. Sprinkles rain out of the balloon onto the ice cream. Then a claw picks up the bowl and sets it on a conveyor belt, where it is sprayed with chocolate syrup.

"It's an ice-cream-sundae machine!"

A cherry rolls down a slide and lands on top of the sundae. Then the machine stops.

"It looks so good!" you exclaim.

The puffles hop up and down, and one brings you three spoons.

"I think they want us to taste," PH says.

As you eat, PH tells you how the brown puffles were discovered.

"I was on the trail of the brown puffles for a while, but I couldn't find them," she says. "Then in 2011, penguins who embarked on the Wilderness Expedition helped me locate this cave. I was so excited to finally see the brown puffles!

They're extremely interesting."

"Definitely," you agree.

You thank the brown puffles for the ice cream and head back to follow the strange tracks. You cross the bay once more and pick up the tracks where you left off.

The tracks take you around the bottom of the cliff and back to a wooded area. At the edge of the trees a small group of puffles are performing what looks like a strange dance.

"Well, isn't that something?" PH says, stopping in her tracks. "I've never seen a dance like that before. I should record this."

She's about to open her backpack when she looks down at the snow and frowns.

"The snow is starting to melt," she realizes. "We might lose those tracks soon. Maybe I shouldn't record this."

**If you stay to witness the dance, go to page 21.**

**If you keep following the tracks, go to page 14.**

"I wonder if that red button opens the door?" you wonder out loud.

"Don't touch it!" PH warns. "That would be too easy. I think that control panel is probably the key to getting in. It looks like there's some kind of code to figure out."

You study the control panel. "There are five shapes. A circle, a square, a triangle, a star, and a rectangle."

"Maybe you have to press them in a certain order?" Jet guesses.

"Let's give it a try," PH says.

You press the shapes in order: circle, square, triangle, star, rectangle. Nothing happens.

"There's got to be a way," Jet says, and he tries another random combination: triangle, star, circle, square, rectangle. Nothing.

"Come on!" Jet says, frustrated. He tries another combination, but that doesn't work, either.

You're thoughtful. "There's got to be some logic to it," you say.

"I agree," PH says. "What's a logical way to order the shapes?"

Then it hits you. "Maybe they're in alphabetical order!"

Jet steps aside, and you carefully touch the shapes in alphabetical order: circle, rectangle, square, star, triangle. You hear a click, and the door swings open.

"That was ace!" PH congratulates you. "Now let's be careful. That door has Herbert's paws all over it."

You all enter the door and find yourself in a chamber with metal walls. A huge machine with wires and tubes fills the space. There are words scrawled on the side: *Herbert's Ice Melter.*

"An ice-melting machine!" PH exclaims. "That pesky polar bear plans to turn all of Club Penguin into a giant swimming pool!"

"We've got to stop him!" you say.

Then you hear a sound coming through the walls of the chamber. It sounds like a flute.

"Chirp!" PH cries, and she pushes through a door on the wall.

In the next room, a little yellow puffle is trapped in a cave. PH quickly uses the tools on her spy phone to pick the lock and grabs the puffle.

"Chirp! Are you okay?" PH asks.

The little yellow puffle nods and jumps out of PH's arms. It hops around on the floor.

"I see," PH says, interpreting the puffle's movements. "You followed Herbert to the cave and then got caught in a booby trap. Is Herbert still here?"

Chirp shakes its head no, and PH turns to you and Jet.

"We've got to try to destroy the machine before he gets back. Let's take a look at it."

The machine is a complicated mess of wires and tubes attached to what looks like a large motor.

"We could pull out all the wires," you suggest.

"Or maybe we should take apart the motor," Jet says.

**If you pull out the wires, go to page 19.**

**If you take apart the motor, go to page 77.**

**CONTINUED FROM PAGE 18.**

Jet's idea appeals to you.

"Let's do it!" you say. "If we can find the puffle herd on our own, it'll be an amazing discovery."

You head down the left-hand path, but you don't get far before there's another fork in the road.

"Which way should we go?" you wonder.

Jet waddles to the center of the fork, where a big tree is growing. Fuzzy, green moss is growing up the right-hand side.

"I read somewhere that moss grows on the north side of the tree," he says. "So I think if we go right, we'll be okay."

You shake your head. "I'm pretty sure moss grows on the south side of the tree. We should go left."

**If you agree with Jet and go right, go to page 31.**

**If you're sure moss grows on the south side of the tree, go to page 55.**

You're curious to see how the big cannon works, so you ask PH to show you how to play *Puffle Launch.* She ushers you behind the cannon and shows you how to work the controls.

"Don't you need to use a puffle to play with?" Jet asks.

PH looks up at the plastic tubing. "Here comes one now."

A red puffle drops from the tube into the cannon. PH fastens a red-and-white helmet on top of its fuzzy head.

"Ready?" PH asks you, and you nod.

*Whoosh!* The cannon shoots the puffle out the window into the blue sky. It lands in a shiny green cannon and immediately is shot out again. The puffle gobbles up Puffle O's and lands in another cannon. Then it automatically shoots out again!

"The object is to reach the flaming hoop at the end of the course, collecting Puffle O's along the way," PH tells you.

The puffle lands in a cannon, but this time doesn't shoot out. The cannon revolves, turning from left to right.

"When the cannon is pointing where you want it, you can launch the puffle," PH instructs.

You wait until the cannon is lined up with the Puffle O's and launch. The red puffle soars through the air, gulping down the round treats as it goes. Then it flies through the flaming hoop.

"Beauty! You finished Level One!" PH exclaims.

The red puffle bounces back through the window. It looks really happy.

"Want to try again?" you ask it, and the puffle nods.

Jet starts flipping the controls. "Try Level Four. There are balloons on that level."

The cannon launches again, and the red puffle soars through the air. This level is a little more challenging. There are big green balloons floating everywhere, and the puffle bounces off them into the cannons.

You do pretty well, and then you come to a tricky spot.

"I'm not sure what to do," you say. "Should I aim for that green balloon or shoot for the cannon next to me?"

"Trust your instincts," PH tells you. "That's the best way to learn."

**If you aim for the green balloon, go to page 17.**

**If you aim for the cannon, go to page 48.**

## CONTINUED FROM PAGE 54.

"Um, I guess I'm creative," you answer.

PH looks thoughtful. "Well, brown puffles are creative because they're always inventing and improving things. And yellow puffles are more artistically creative. They like to paint, make music, and perform."

You've always dreamed of being onstage, so the choice is easy.

"I'll go with a yellow puffle!" you decide.

PH grins. "Nice choice. Let's get you to the Pet Shop!"

A short while later you're sitting in the Pizza Parlor with Jet and your new yellow puffle. It's at the piano, playing a happy song.

"It sounds like your new puffle is happy you adopted it," Jet remarks.

"Are you kidding?" you ask. "I'm the happy one. I finally have a puffle to call my own!"

## THE END

"I like to have fun," you say.

"Who doesn't?" PH asks with a grin. "So I can think of three good choices for you. Purple puffles love to go to parties and dance. Orange puffles are curious and eager to try new things. And green puffles are mischievous."

You remember how the green puffle at the Beacon got you to chase him.

"I think I'll go with a green puffle!" you say.

"Then let's go back to the Pet Shop!" PH tells you.

A short while later you and Jet are walking through the Plaza while your green puffle flies next to you wearing a propeller hat.

"I think you should call it Jet," Jet says.

"Why not?" you say. "It flies around, and you did help me today. Along with PH."

Your green puffle flies in front of you, blows a raspberry, and flies off. You and Jet laugh, and then you chase it. Owning a green puffle is definitely going to be fun!

**THE END**

# CONTINUED FROM PAGE 39.

"Let's just blow it once and see what happens," Jet suggests.

*Tweet!* You go outside and blow the whistle, and the sound bounces off the mountains. Things are tense as you and Jet quietly wait for something to happen. And then you see it—a green blur coming across the snow toward you. And it looks like it's flying!

As the blur gets closer, you realize it's a green puffle wearing a red-and-white propeller cap. When the puffle reaches you and Jet, it hovers expectantly.

"Are you an Elite Puffle?" you ask, and the puffle nods. "Then we need your help. PH fell into some kind of trapdoor. Come on, we'll show you."

The green puffle follows you into the tunnel. When you point out the trapdoor, it flies around it curiously for a moment. Then it goes zipping out of the cave.

"Maybe it's getting help," you suggest.

You nervously wait once more until you see the green puffle return with a red

penguin wearing a black suit and dark sunglasses.

"I'll take it from here," he says, brushing past you and Jet. "This is official EPF business. Come on, Flit."

He motions to the green puffle and then disappears inside the tunnel.

You're disappointed. "I wish I could help," you tell Jet. "It's my fault that PH is trapped down there."

"We'd better leave this to the pros," Jet says. "And anyway, in a few weeks we can take the EPF test ourselves."

"Cool," you say. "Who knows? Maybe one day we'll get to see PH again!"

## THE END

# CONTINUED FROM PAGE 61.

"A black O'berry," PH says, her eyes wide. "I've never seen one before! This is amazing."

She looks at the green puffle. "Can you show us where you got this?"

In response, the green puffle zooms off into the trees. You, PH, and Jet take off running after it. You're not sure if the little guy is teasing you or just too fast for his own good because you can barely keep up.

You're moving so fast that you don't see a rock on the path in front of you. *Bam!* You trip, landing beakfirst in the snow.

PH and Jet rush to help you up. As PH bends down, she pauses.

"What do you know? That looks like a puffle track," she says.

As you get up and brush off the snow, PH bends down to get a closer look. Then she takes out a camera and starts snapping photos.

"I'm not sure, but it looks like the puffle that made this track has a tail," she says, pointing to a short line attached to the puffle-shaped track. "Then again, it could just be a mark in the snow

I'd have to find more tracks to be sure."

She glances down the path. "But if we stop to do that, we'll lose the green puffle. What should we do?"

If you decide to follow the green puffle, go to page 45.

If you decide to follow the strange puffle track, go to page 58.

# CONTINUED FROM PAGE 66.

"I think we should be careful," PH warns. "The machine might be booby-trapped, too."

"Then let's try the motor," you say. "That looks safer."

PH takes out her spy phone, presses a button, and a wrench pops out.

"Cool," Jet says. "I can't wait until we're both Agents so we can get spy phones."

"You both would make great Agents," PH says with a smile. "Now let's bust up this machine!"

You and Jet use the wrench to unscrew the bolts holding the parts of the motor together. PH takes a burlap sack from her backpack and stuffs them inside.

"We don't want Herbert to be able to put this back together," she says.

Then you notice a bolt that seems to be holding up the base of the machine. After a few turns of the wrench, the bolt pops loose and the machine collapses in a heap of groaning metal.

Jet high-fives you. "Nice job!"

"Great work," PH says. "Now let's get

back to HQ and file a report."

You and Jet have never been inside EPF headquarters before, and it's exciting to see all of the computer screens buzzing with activity and Agents in dark glasses waddling around. PH leaves for a moment and comes back with a blue penguin wearing a lab coat.

"This is G," she says. "I told him how you both helped me."

G smiles and hands each of you a spy phone. "You've both proven that you can be EPF Agents," he says. "And I'd like to reward you as well."

He hands you each a pair of goggles with green lenses.

"They're Dark Vision Goggles," he says. "You can use them to see in the dark. They're from our Elite Gear collection. You've earned them."

You and Jet put on your goggles and grin.

"Awesome!" you say.

## THE END

## CONTINUED FROM PAGE 14.

"Let's climb the tree," you say. "I'm not sure any of us can fit down that hole."

"Good point," PH agrees. "Here, Jet and I will give you a boost."

Penguins might not be known for their tree-climbing ability, but with the help of your friends you hoist yourself onto the first tree branch. The next branch is within reach, so you climb that one and then the next one. Soon you have a great view of the tree's top branches—but there's no sign of a puffle, strange or otherwise.

You're about to climb down when you spot something in a high branch on a nearby tree. A brown puffle is stuck in the branch, tangled up in what look like the strings of a parachute. The poor puffle looks frightened.

"Guys! There's a puffle in trouble!" you yell as you quickly climb down the tree. PH and Jet follow you to the tree where the brown puffle is trapped.

"It must have been experimenting with a new flying craft and had to parachute to safety when it malfunctioned," PH guesses. "Can

79

you help me get it down?"

"No problem!" you say, and PH hands you a small pair of scissors. Then you and Jet climb up the tree until you reach the puffle.

"Hang in there, little guy," you say, gently reaching out to hold the puffle in your flipper. Jet cuts the string, freeing the puffle, and you both climb down.

PH grins. "Great job! You two will make great puffle handlers some day."

You look down at the little brown puffle, who's shivering in your flipper. "You're safe now," you say. "Would you like to come live with me in my igloo?"

The brown puffle nods happily, and you let out a cheer.

"Yay! I just adopted my first puffle!"

## THE END